His Choice

A Dante's Circle Novella

By
Carrie Ann Ryan

His Choice copyright © 2013 Carrie Ann Ryan

His Choice

As the youngest son of Lucifer, Fawkes has long since known what paths his future could take. He could follow his father's footsteps, stealing the souls of humans and slowly lose his own, or starve himself and wither away until he finds his true half and forms a bond that can not only save his life, but his soul.

Leslie Masterson's life has been one torment after another. A submissive wolf, she's tried to hide in the shadows of her Pack and find the will to live another day. After her brother—the man who has beaten her verbally and physically her entire life—is killed when he challenges the Alpha,

Leslie finally sees a path to freedom.

It only takes one look between the two for them to know that they could be the answer to each other's prayers, but some of the Pack isn't ready to let Leslie go. It will take the strength of a fiery demon from hell and the love of a submissive wolf to overcome not only their past, but their chance at a future.

Dante's Circle Characters

With an ever growing list of characters in each book, I know that it might seem like there are too many to remember. Well don't worry; here is a list for you so you don't forget. Not all are seen in this exact book, but here are the ones you've met so far. As the series progresses, the list will as well.

Happy reading!

Agda—Brownie council leader.

Agnes—Sole female on the Angelic council.

Amara Young—One of the seven lightning struck women. Works at an inn. Has a past that is very secretive.

Ambrose Griffin—Warrior angel, Shade's mentor. Father to Laura *(deceased)* and Nathan *(deceased)*, husband to Ilianya *(deceased)*. Mate to Balin and Jamie, story told in *Her Warriors' Three Wishes*.

Azel—Black-winged angel. Striker's third in command.

Balin Drake—Non-soul devouring demon, son of Pyro. Mate to Jamie and Ambrose, story told in *Her Warriors' Three Wishes*.

Becca Quinn—One of the seven lightning struck women. Works as a bartender at Dante's Circle. Mate to Hunter Brooks, story told in *An Unlucky Moon*.

Bryce—Lily's ex-fiancee.

Caine—Angelic council leader.

Cora—Shade's ex-fiancé *(deceased)*.

Dante Bell—Dragon shifter. Owner of Dante's Circle.

Eli—Bakery Owner.

Eliana Sawyer—One of the seven lightning struck women. Works as a welder.

Faith Sanders—One of the seven lightning struck women. Works as a photographer.

Fawkes—Demon, son of Lucifer, friend of Balin. Story told in *His Choice* (Found in the Anthology *Ever After*).

Fury—Leader of the demon council.

Glenn—Lily's sleazy ex-boss.

Hunter Brooks—Wolf and Beta of the Nocturne Pack. Met Ambrose, Jamie, and Balin in hell during the demon games. Mate to Becca, story told in *An Unlucky Moon*.

Ilianya—*(deceased)* Sister to Shade, wife to Ambrose.

Jamie Bennett—One of the seven lightning struck women. Bookstore owner and lover of romance. Mate to Ambrose and Balin, story told in *Her Warriors' Three Wishes*.

Kobal—Old djinn council member, ally to Pyro.

Law—Gray-winged angel, Striker's second in command.
Lily Banner—One of the seven lightning struck women. Worked as a lab chemist in solid-state NMR. OCD and quirky. Mate to Shade, story told in *Dust of My Wings*.
Lucifer—Infamous demon from hell and Fawkes' father.
Laura—*(deceased)* Daughter of Ambrose.
Nadie Morgan—One of the seven lightning struck woman. Works as a school teacher.
Nathan—*(deceased)* Son of Amborse.
Pyro—Demon from hell, father to Balin.
Shade Griffin—Warrior angel, ex-fiance to Cora, brother to Illianya, mate to Lily Banner, story told in *Dust of My Wings*.
Striker—Angelic council member, leader of the rebels.

Temperance—New Djinn council leader.
Thad—Co-worker of Lily's. Had a crush on her.
Timmy—10 year old brownie.

CHAPTER ONE

"You're a disgrace to the name Devil, son," Lucifer spat as he paced the long dungeon. "You had such promise and then you've thrown it all away. Or at least, you're planning on it. Don't lie to me. I know all."

Fawkes looked up through the blood running down his face,

stinging his eyes, and lifted a lip in a sneer.

He was twenty years old—young to most but a grown man to others—and yet the way his father treated him it was as if *he* was the adolescent who needed a good scolding.

Not that his father had ever acted the caring paternal figure.

"You're the actual Devil, Dad," Fawkes said, his voice slightly hoarse from screaming. Sometimes the screaming helped the pain, even if it did annoy him Lucifer enjoyed it so much. "I'm just one of your many sons."

Lucifer rolled his eyes—a gesture that made him look as immature as he acted—then ran a hand over his red horns that stood a foot out from his head—the exact matching pair to Fawkes'.

"You're my last son, Fawkes. The others are either fierce

warriors and soul eaters or dead. None of them however, ever chose the path you're looking at. No son of mine will. They all died in battle or because they were idiots. I won't let you sully my good name. It's time for you to make your choice and eat the souls of humans."

Though Fawkes was chained to a wall in his father's favorite torture room, he didn't feel threatened by the man humans feared more that the things that went bump in the night. Actually, his father *was* the thing that went bump in the night. Lucifer just wanted Fawkes to fall into his deadly footsteps, taking souls and becoming dark.

Fawkes wasn't sure he wanted to do that though.

He'd seen what the other possibility could be and, frankly, that looked better.

Harsher.

Deadlier.

Once a demon reached twenty, he had a year to reach a decision before his life started to fade. Demons needed souls or a mating bond in order to survive. Without souls, they would die slowly and painfully. Once they reached their three hundredth birthday, they'd fade from existence—excruciatingly. They only had that first year though to take their first soul, or they'd harm themselves to the point that they'd need a true half—the one person, or persons in a triad's case, that was meant for them and would create the perfect mating bond—in order to survive.

Since demons didn't find their true halves with other demons—a punishment for their killing existence—they had to venture out into the human and other realms in order to find the person—or persons—who would not only be part of them, but save their lives. Demons could mate with each other and create more demon offspring, like his father had done with the many women who'd given birth to Lucifer's progeny, but they would never find that perfect...peace within that mating.

Another demon, Balin, had been one of the few to actually choose against becoming evil. The other demon had almost died because he'd refused to do what almost all other demons had done in order to survive. It was only because Balin had found Jamie *and* Ambrose that he'd survived at all.

Now Fawkes was old enough to make his choice.

Lucifer narrowed his eyes. "Are you even listening?"

Fawkes blinked. "Uh...yeah?"

Lucifer spat then let the fire running through his veins rage from his palms. He spent his energy toward the wall, scorching a line of black soot in an arch before fisting his hands, letting the fire burn itself out.

Fawkes had to learn that handy trick.

"You have less than six months until you have to choose. If you don't take your first soul, you'll waste away until you find your true half. It doesn't matter if you take souls after that because you'll still fade away. That's what Balin didn't understand before and that's why you *will* take a soul. Now."

"It's *my* choice Dad. Mine."

"I'll do what Pyro to Balin and keep you here until you have to make the correct choice," Lucifer threatened.

"Pyro was a sadistic bastard."

Lucifer gave him a bland look. "I'm the Devil, son. No one

is worse than me. It would do you good to remember that."

Fawkes held back a groan. His father had to be the most conceited demon out there. *No* demon was allowed to be stronger or fiercer than him.

"Yes, you're more of a sadistic bastard than Pyro ever was," he deadpanned.

Lucifer blinked slowly then pressed a button on the wall. The chains attached to the manacles on Fawkes' wrists pulled up and turned, forcing his gaze to the opposite wall and leaving his back to his father's ministrations.

This couldn't end well.

The first crack of the whip was a familiar sting. He'd been beaten all his life, but not to the point others in his father's *care* had been. He was still whole, still himself.

He knew others out there hadn't fared as well.

HIS CHOICE

Lucifer snapped the whip again, the pain arching across Fawkes' back a heated flame. He gritted his teeth and let his father finish his ministrations before finally Lucifer gave up.

"I'd lock you up but the last thing I need is the other demons thinking I can't take care of one of my own," Lucifer spat. "You'll have to make the choice yourself, but if you make the wrong one..."

Fawkes didn't answer his father's unspoken words. No matter what, the Devil wanted his due and Fawkes would have to take the blame. He just didn't know if he could last as long as Balin had.

He thought of the angel and demon pair that had promised him sanctuary in the human realm. If he went to them now, he might be condemning himself to death, but that might be better than what he'd do once he took a soul.

One didn't come back from that whole.

His father left without another word, slamming his hand into the button on his way out the door. The manacles around Fawkes' wrists opencd and he slammed onto the floor. He ran his tongue over his molars to make sure he didn't crack one with that jolt then stood on shaky legs. He'd been hanging for a few days and his body had weakened just enough that he knew he needed to either leave the hell realm soon or do something he might regret.

He looked down at his leather pants and boots and shrugged. They would have to do in the human realm because he wasn't about head back to his room and try to get his belongings. He had a feeling if he happened to cross

Lucifer's path again, his father might not be so easy-going and trap him in a dungeon.

Again.

With conscious thought, he forced his human glamour over his body, his horns disappearing from this head. He'd have to make an effort to hide the red flecks in his black eyes, but maybe Balin would be able to help him with that. Fawkes had only ever been to the human realm a few times and that was only on training missions so he could learn how to blend in if necessary.

Despite what other Houses of demons might want to do, he knew one of the most important things he could learn was to keep the supernatural secret. Humans were far more dangerous when they knew the truth about what lay hidden within other realms.

Using some of the last energy he had since he was so freaking hungry, he opened a portal to the human realm. Thankfully, he knew where Ambrose, Jamie, and Balin lived so he could make sure the portal ended in their backyard, rather than in someone else's home. He let his scent signature seep along the portal so the triad would know who was coming and stepped through. The last thing he needed was to end up on the wrong end of Balin's sword because he hadn't announced himself. Plus, Fawkes was unarmed thanks to his dad— not something he truly wanted to be.

He stepped through, the burning fire surrounding him licking at him like hungry flames. It didn't hurt any worse that what his father had done to him recently, so he didn't care.

As the last of the flames died away he blinked open his eyes and smiled.

"It's about time you showed up," Ambrose said. He stood in the backyard of his home, his arms folded over his chest and a frown on his face, though there was no hiding the mix of laughter and concern in his eyes.

"I was tied up," Fawkes explained. From the look on Ambrose's face, he had a feeling the warrior angel knew *exactly* what he meant by that.

"Are you here for good?"

Fawkes shrugged. "I'm not sure yet."

"Ambrose, stop interrogating the boy and let him come inside," Jamie said from the back door.

Fawkes smiled and pushed past Ambrose to sweep Jamie in his arms. She laughed and wrapped her arms around his neck as he inhaled her scent. He'd helped save her once before and now she was going to try to save him.

Something along her scent triggered the protectiveness within him and he froze.

"You're pregnant."

Jamie smiled full out and nodded. "Yes, Becca is as well."

Fawkes remembered hearing about Jamie and her six girlfriends who had all been struck by lightning. They were all now—or would be soon—supernaturals in their own right, rather than humans.

"Balin and Ambrose are actually letting you walk around now? I'd have thought they'd wrap you in bubble wrap and force you to sit the entire time."

"Don't think it hasn't crossed my mind," Balin said as he walked up behind Jamie. "Now get your paws off my mate."

Fawkes grinned then leaned to kiss Jamie on the cheek. She laughed while Balin *and* Ambrose each growled in turn.

Hell, he'd needed this—the teasing and laughter. He wanted the smiles and happiness that he saw on the other demon's face. It could happen for Fawkes, he knew that, but it would be a long journey.

Balin frowned. "You've made your choice, haven't you?"

Fawkes shook his head. "No, not yet. I have time, but I wanted, no *needed* to see what else was out there."

Jamie took his hand and led him into the triad's home. "Go take a shower and get into some of Balin's clothes since you can't walk around in just leather pants in broad daylight while in the human realm."

"I don't know babe, humans are just as weird as everyone else," Balin teased.

Jamie rolled her eyes and put her hand protectively on her stomach. "Shut it. Go show Fawkes what he can wear and the guest bedroom that he can stay in."

Fawkes opened his mouth to say something but Jamie held up her hand.

"You're staying with us, at least for the night. If you want to go somewhere else to roam or learn about what this choice means later, sure. Right now though, you're staying here and eating dinner with us. Hunter and Becca will be here soon to eat and I'm sure they'll want to see you."

Fawkes nodded, remembering the animalistic wolf, Hunter. He'd also helped save him as well and had heard that the wolf had mated Becca, Jamie's friend.

Balin squeezed his shoulder, forcing Fawkes' gaze to his. "Everything will be okay. You know that right?"

Fawkes nodded but knew he was lying. It wasn't a choice that came easily to a demon. Sure, if he were human, not taking souls and slowing dying without knowing if he'd ever find his true half wouldn't seem like as tough a choice.

He wasn't human though.

He was the son of the Devil himself and had to make his choices on his own.

He could do it if he had to, but he didn't know if he wanted to.

What kind of person did that make him?

Oh yeah, a demon.

He nodded toward the others then followed Balin to the guest room where he'd be staying for the time being. After he took a shower and put on Balin's extra jeans and button down, he looked in the mirror and smiled.

He looked almost human. Who knew?

"Stop trying to look pretty and get your ass out here," Balin called from other part of the house and Fawkes rolled his eyes.

Balin had always been like a big brother to him—more so than his actual blood brothers. The other demon had shown him how to fight, how to use a sword, and how to protect himself from others who knew that killing the son of Lucifer would exalt them into legends.

He walked into the living room to find Hunter with his arm wrapped around a beautiful redhead who had to be Becca sitting on the couch.

Hunter smiled at him, though really, on the wolf it looked more like a threat than a true smile.

"Good to see you, Fawkes."

Becca grinned and stood up to give him hug. She smelled of sweetness and growth from the child in her womb. He looked over her shoulder at Hunter's glare and snorted.

"It's nice to meet you, Becca, but you better pull back a bit or your mate will kill me. Slowly."

Becca threw her head back and laughed. "Yeah, that sounds a bit right. Don't worry though, he won't kill you."

"Maybe maim," Jamie added in. "Only slightly though."

"We made fajitas and all the fixings so it's pretty much serve yourself at the table," Balin said as he handed over a beer to the non-pregnant people in the room.

Fawkes took a sip and winced at the unfamiliar bitter taste.

"How is it I've never had one of these before?"

Hunter snorted. "Are you even old enough in the human realm?"

"Shit, I forgot about that," Balin said as he reached out to take it back.

Fawkes raised a brow. "I'm a demon and almost twenty-one. I have more to worry about than those few months."

Ambrose just shook his head and sighed. "I'm not in the mood to deal with human politics. I've seen enough of it in my time."

"That would be a *long* time, right honey?" Balin teased.

"You'll pay for that later," Ambrose growled.

The two males' eyes darkened and Fawkes had a feeling he'd be using some earplugs later that night to block out any noise from the master bedroom.

Fawkes watched the others make their fajitas and copied them, using extra salsa like Balin since apparently demons liked it hot. The spices mingled on his tongue and he washed it down with his beer, wondering how the hell he'd got here.

"What's wrong, Fawkes?" Jamie asked.

"Nothing really," he lied.

She narrowed her eyes and he laughed softly. "I don't know what I'm doing. I left my dad's chamber without really thinking about the consequences." The table got quiet at the thought of what must have happened in the chamber, but he didn't elaborate. He didn't need to, considering what each person at the table had been through on their own.

"I know when you left hell before, Balin, you all gave me the opportunity to leave if I needed to, but I didn't know if I was ready. I don't know what I'm doing."

"Do you want to take souls?" Balin asked point blank. "Do you want to end human lives because that's how you think demons should live?"

"No. I don't want to kill anyone who doesn't deserve it."

"You've answered your own question then," Ambrose added. "You're confused because you've been on the path that's easy and paved with your father's intentions. I know that isn't the one you want. It might kill you, but you'd have been lost to us and yourself if you'd taken the other path. You're here for a reason, Fawkes."

Fawkes swallowed hard and looked at his half eaten plate. "What do I do?"

Jamie reached out and gripped his hand. "Stay with us. We'll help you anyway you can.

You have years, Fawkes, years to find your mate."

"You won't be in the same position I was in either," Balin added. "You won't be forced to go back to hell. Lucifer has no place in the human realm, no matter how hard he tries. You can travel to the other realms as well, at least most of them, and look for your mate."

Fawkes snorted. "So spend my whole life searching for someone who might not exist?"

Balin narrowed his eyes. "At least you'll have the option unlike others."

Fawkes nodded, remembering that Balin's father had forced him to stay in hell until he'd lost enough energy that he hadn't been able to go to the other realms to search for his mate.

"Enjoy life, Fawkes," Hunter said, surprising Fawkes that the wolf would speak of enjoyment when he hadn't any before he'd met Becca. "Don't take the time you have for granted. You'll have years to find her. Fate will provide, you have to believe in that."

"It looks like I've made my choice," Fawkcs whispered, knowing he'd made his choice the moment he'd left hell in the first place.

Jamie squeezed his hand. "You've decided to be good. That's okay, Fawkes. We'll help you live."

Fawkes looked at the people who had welcomed him without reservations and blinked hard. He might have made one choice, but that didn't mean there weren't others to come. He still had to find the one woman for him, the one that could create the mating bond and provide enough energy that he wouldn't fade away.

The idea of fading away though paled in comparison to what he'd have to do if he chose souls over the humanity that he wanted to emulate.

He'd taken the first step. Now he just had to find her.

CHAPTER TWO

Six Months Later

L eslie Masterson wanted a mate.
Badly.

Her wolf wanted one even more than she did.

The human part of her wanted that perfect mate for life. Sure, had a certain itch that she needed to scratch, but that wasn't the point. She'd had sex before, come on, she was forty after all, but it had been way too long.

At least five years if she was counting.

Not that she was counting.

Daily.

It wasn't her fault really. Her brother, Dorian, had forbade all others to even look at her unless it was for his own political gain. He had been part of the Nocturne Pack's council—the group of five families who had tried to take over the Alpha and Beta.

Thankfully Hunter, the Beta, had won the dominance battle against her brother and had stopped a likely war within their own Pack.

Her brother had died in the process yet Leslie couldn't muster up much pity or sadness for that. She didn't know exactly what that said about her, but honestly, she didn't care anymore.

She was a submissive wolf—a wolf who held the lower end of the spectrum in terms of dominance. Her wolf loved to let others control her and tell her what to do, but it wasn't something wrong like what others thought. Her wolf wanted to be part of a relationship with another wolf where the more dominate wolf would take care of her.

Being a submissive wolf meant the dominant wolves had others to protect and care for. That way their own issues with dominance would be soothed and the submissive wolf would be able to care for their dominant wolf in other ways.

The human part of Leslie wasn't as submissive as her wolf, but she too wanted someone to care for her like she wanted to care for them. She wasn't as strong as other wolves and knew she needed the protection. It was simple biology. She had other strengths and could protect those in her care if needed.

She just happened to be on the lower end of the power totem pole.

Normally it wouldn't have been an issue but because Dorian had taken advantage of that, she'd spent almost her whole life in the shadows. She'd begged her brother to allow her more freedom and cursed herself when she realized her wolf needed permission for that freedom.

Now Dorian was dead and she was free.

Or at least as free as she could be within the Pack den without a mate.

It's not like she necessarily needed a mate to live, no that would be idiotic of fate. She wanted to move on though. It had been over six months since her brother died and yet the others were still weary of her.

Some still thought she was part of the conspiracy to take over the Pack because of the blood running through her veins. Others had the idea that because she was a submissive, she didn't matter as much.

The latter her Alpha and Beta were working on.

Their Pack had almost broken and were wrong in the way they were thinking on some things. She'd been told submissives were to be treasured, yet that wasn't how it was done now.

Or at least for the past few years. Things were changing, albeit slowly.

Too slowly for her though because she was alone.

Sure, she'd made some friends and was a little more open, but not enough. She wasn't nearly independent enough for her own taste, but that was for safety now, rather than her own choices. She had to live with Hunter and his mate—and her friend—Becca because it still wasn't completely safe for her on her own.

People wanted revenge for what had happened and she was the easy scape goat for those who didn't look beyond the surface.

Leslie walked past a group of males and lowered her head on instinct. They were all more dominant than her and in the past—before the attacks—she'd have been able to walk past them no problem. But after years of living with Dorian's abuse, she didn't trust herself.

The males growled at her and she winced.

"Wait up, Leslie," one of them said and she turned as quick as she could to follow his call.

If the group had been healthy, they would have assured her stance quickly by offering her a hug or touch to show her how loved she was in the Pack.

This group wasn't like that.

Hell, she missed Becca and Hunter already and it had only been a fcw hours since she'd seen them.

"Oh, hello Colin," she answered, keeping her gaze on his chin rather than try to meet his eyes.

He reached out and ran a finger along her cheek. Her wolf nudged against her skin then let out a shuddered breath at the contact. It wasn't sexual or territorial.

No, this was Pack.

This was something she needed.

She'd already been touch-starved before Dorian had betrayed the Pack openly. After that almost all others had shunned her. If it hadn't been for Hunter, Becca, Liam, and Alec, she would have died. The latter two, council members in their own right, had taken her under their wing much like they would a baby sister.

There was no mating in their eyes and she didn't blame them. She didn't feel anything for them but deep respect and guilt that her brother had threatened their way of life.

That seemed par for the course these days.

"Your wolf needs touch," Colin growled, causing the other men around him to growl as well.

Her wolf cowered and she cursed herself. She was stronger than this, darn it. Why couldn't her wolf see this?

"I know," she answered honestly. "I'm working on it." It was just really hard to do when most of the Pack wanted nothing to do with her and the rest scared the crap out of her. Alec and Liam could only do so much and she wasn't about to snuggle up to Hunter daily while Becca nursed their newborn baby girl.

"Your bloodlines are pure, Leslie," Colin continued. "You'd make someone a good mate."

She blinked.

Bloodlines.

Seriously?

It always came back to bloodlines. Dorian had been fanatic about it and look what had happened. She knew the blood running through her veins was of the finest families in the Pack's history, but considering what had happened recently, she hadn't thought it mattered.

She didn't care about who her family's family was. She didn't care about purity.

Colin, apparently, did.

"You don't complain and you do as you're told," Colin continued. "A male would be pleased to have you for your child bearing alone. You're quite fuckable as well. I don't think it would be a chore to slam my cock into you during full moons. I'm sure that you'll like the others too. After all, you're a pureblood with tradition in your veins. You know the full moon hunts require us to either take flesh or fuck. I'm sure you understand with the female shortage in our Pack, that any mate of ours would have to be shared with the lot of us. You'll enjoy it."

Leslie blinked again.

Never had such romantic words been spoken, she thought dryly.

Her wolf backed away from his touch and she lifted a lip in a snarl—so unlike her. "Remove your hand."

Colin's brows rose but he didn't move. He pinched her chin and forced her to meet his gaze. "What was that?"

She gulped and cursed herself. Fear wafted from her and she wanted to slink into a corner and hide. It wasn't her fault she was a submissive but dominants weren't supposed to lord their power over her. They weren't supposed to make her cower in fear.

They were supposed to love her.

They were supposed to protect her so she could protect herself.

When had everything gone to hell?

"Let me go, Colin." Her voice shook and she lowered her eyes because of his wolf, but she still spoke. She was stronger than he thought. Or at least she hoped.

He pinched harder and leaned down so his mouth was almost over hers. Those in the Pack kissed in friendly ways to show affection often, but that wasn't what Colin wanted to do. He wanted to prove his dominance over her in front of his friends.

She hated that he made her hate herself.

"You think you can talk to me like that? You're nothing but a useless bitch who needs a good fuck to get over herself," he spat.

Her wolf growled even as she cowered. "You don't know me, Colin. None of you do. I won't be mating with any of you. Our Alpha won't force me."

Colin narrowed his eyes. "He can't watch you always."

"No, but she has others on her side other than the Alpha," Hunter growled as he stalked toward her.

Inwardly, she relaxed though she did her best not to show that to Colin. She couldn't afford to show any more weakness that she already had.

"Stay out of this, Beta," Colin warned.

"Get your hands off of her before I tear them from your arms," Liam warned as he came up from behind, Alec, like always, by his side.

Her wolf nudged along her skin, desperate to touch the more dominant wolves around her who treated her with respect.

Colin pulled back but not without shooting her dirty look. "She's a pureblood. She's made for mating. You can't protect her from that."

Alec shook his head and crossed his arms over his chest. "Leslie is a person. Stop acting like you own her and all the females in the Pack."

Colin snorted. "Maybe if I did, we wouldn't be running out of women."

Hunter moved so quickly she didn't even see him. One second she was standing in front of Colin, the next she was behind Alec as Hunter had Colin on the ground, one knee on his chest and his forearm against his neck.

Liam stood, claws out, ready to take on Colin's friends, though the other wolves looked reluctant to fight three of the strongest wolves in the Pack.

"Our Pack lost what was most precious to us when wolves like you decided to try to take over. The submissives don't feel safe and others don't want to mate outside the species. That is what's killing us, not leniency. Speak to Leslie or anyone else like that again and I'll gut you where you stand."

"You'll destroy all of us," Colin rasped.

"You've already tried," Hunter said simply then punched the other wolf in the face before standing up.

Leslie cocked a brow at that and Hunter shrugged.

"I slipped," he replied.

She bit her tongue to hold back a snort. The last thing she needed to do was laugh and start a full-out brawl over hurt feelings.

Already she could tell her wolf was happier and more confident with dominant wolves who not only respected her, but treated her as if she were worth something more than breeding. If only everyone treated her this way and maybe she'd get out of her funk.

Maybe she could even find a mate.

Okay, that might be a long shot, but she had to have hope.

Without that, what was the point?

"Go home," Hunter ordered Colin's crew. "If I catch you sniffing around any of the submissives who don't want your attention, I won't be so nice."

The other wolves glared, but left, knowing that Hunter, Alec, and Liam were stronger than them by far.

Alec reached out and gripped her hand before smiling— something the wolf rarely did. "Are you all right?"

Leslie nodded. "Yes. I'm sorry you had to see that."

Liam cursed and pulled her into his arms, inhaling her scent like he needed to know she was okay. "You should not have had to deal with that at all," he whispered. "You're family, Leslie. Never forget."

She rolled her eyes, but smiled at his tone. As if she could ever forget these men thought of her as the little sister they never had.

"I won't." She pulled back and cupped his cheek with her palm. "You're a good man, Liam. You need a mate."

His eyes darkened before darting to Alec and back to her. Like a good friend, she didn't mention the slip.

"Do you want a mate, Leslie?" Alec asked behind her.

"Are you asking?" she teased.

Alec and Liam sputtered as Hunter burst out laughing. "You've been hanging out with Becca too much I think," the Beta said.

Leslie grinned, surprised she could so quickly after the confrontation with Colin. "Your mate is awesome and you know it."

Hunter smiled a smile of a deeply satisfied male. "You don't have to tell me that. Were you on your way home?" he asked and she held back a wince.

Home.

Not hers, not really. She lived with Hunter, Becca, and their new baby Hazel. She needed a home of her own but she hadn't been ready before.

Soon though.

Soon.

"Yep, I'm on my way home now."

Hunter nodded then held out his arm like a gentleman from another time. "Then let me take you there. I'm on my way to check on Hazel."

Leslie bit back another laugh. She loved that this very alpha wolf had no qualms about showing how much he loved his mate and newborn baby daughter. He showed them both off every chance he had and didn't care who snickered.

She had a feeling though that when Hazel got a little older he wouldn't be showing her off as much considering how boys reacted in their Pack to girls.

"Are you going to ever let me hold that little girl?" Liam asked as the four of them made it toward the Beta's home.

Hunter growled. "You did when she was first born and joked about squeezing her because she was so cute. You won't be holding her again."

Alec snorted then grinned. "I'm allowed to hold her, right?"

Liam punched Alec in the arm and Leslie leaned into Hunter as they walked. This was the family she had, not the one that she was born with, but the one that had been made around her.

HIS CHOICE

She didn't have a mate nor did she have blood relations, but she'd take what she could.

She'd find her mate one day. She just had to believe.

CHAPTER THREE

"Blow out your candles, Fawkes," Jamie ordered as she clapped like a teenager, rather than the new mom she was.

Fawkes grinned and did as he was told, blowing out all twenty-one candles from his birthday cake. Thankfully Lily, Jamie's friend, had made the cake and brought it to the bar Dante's

Circle. He wasn't sure he'd been able to stomach Jamie's try at baking.

Not that he'd tell her or her two very protective mates that.

He had more self-preservation than that.

When he pulled back he forced a bigger smile at the crew in front of him. All of Jamie's friends, their mates' and Dante, the bar owner stood or sat around the table, some with their babies in their arms. All of them had that same look of tension, fear, and uncertainty.

He might have thought he'd made his choice six months ago when he'd stayed in the human realm to find his mate, but in reality, it would be much harder from here on out.

He wouldn't be able to just stand back and let the choice be made for him. He'd have to stand and fight against his own instincts. The year long wait from twenty-one to twenty-two would bring out his demon in truth.

His body would war against itself, begging for human souls and taking out almost all his energy before he found his equilibrium and the choice was made permanent.

Fawkes would have to be on alert the entire time and make sure he didn't give into the temptation of being a true demon. As soon as the year was up, he'd be able to consciously breathe again and know that he'd taken the harder route. He'd then have until his three hundredth birthday to find his true half and mate before he died.

He'd already searched for her within the human realm and had come up short. Though he'd known it wouldn't have been that easy, some part of him had wished it so.

He might have been younger than everyone in the room, but he still wanted to have that special person and start his future. Watching Balin fall for not only Jamie, but Ambrose too had changed something in him.

Now he just had to find his true half while fighting his inner demon's right for control.

A walk in the park.

"What did you wish for?" Becca asked as she kissed her baby's forehead. Hunter had Becca in his lap so he could hold the both of them with ease.

"If he told you that, he'd lose his wish," Jamie said as she leaned into Ambrose. She too sat in his lap while Balin held their baby.

It was getting really domestic, really fast. Even Lily was holding her child as Shade made funny faces to get them both to laugh.

"So, have you decided what realm you're visiting next?" Nadie, the quiet blonde in the corner asked.

Fawkes nodded and looked down at his fisted hands. He'd spend the next year going from realm to realm, exploring and looking for his mate. After that year was over, he'd probably continue to do the same, though he'd find a place to live permanently.

"I wish I could take you to the angelic realm," Ambrose added.

The demon and angelic realms were the only ones with true blockades that he was aware of. Demons couldn't step foot in the heavens and angels could walk through hell.

That didn't mean they didn't try. Ambrose, after all, had made his way through hell with the help of Dante, a dragon, to find Jamie.

That's how Fawkes had met the angel.

"It's okay, Ambrose," Fawkes replied. "It's not as if angels and demons mate daily. You and Balin seem to be the exception."

Balin grinned. "I like being the exception. Now stop stalling, where are you going next?"

Fawkes let out a breath and shrugged. "I don't know. I feel like I'm on an endless path with no hope in sight. I don't like not knowing what will happen. I don't want to be on anyone's charity. I want to be my own man, but I don't know how to do that either."

Hunter nodded then kissed Becca's head. "You'll come with us then," the wolf ordered, surprising Fawkes.

"What now?"

"You're twenty-one, you're not supposed to know what you want to do with the rest of your existence with such firm clarity you don't feel fear," Becca answered. "You're supposed to feel lost. You've made a huge decision to stay on a path you weren't ready for. You save my friends' and my mate's life so let us repay you for that by taking care of you as much as you'll let us."

Fawkes swallowed the lump in his throat and nodded. "You think I'll find my mate within the Pack?"

Hunter shrugged. "Who knows, but it'll be better than staying here feeling sorry for yourself."

"Thanks for making me feel better," he said dryly.

"It's not my job to make you feel like rainbows and unicorn shit," Hunter replied. "It's my job to take care of my mate, my child, my Pack and my debts. You need guidance and structure, fine, we'll help with that. You'll spend the next century searching for something you might not find, but you'll spend it with people who care about you. Stop feeling sorry for yourself and find something to live for. If you don't, then what was the point of making your choice?"

Those were more words than he'd ever heard from the wolf but they were true.

Fawkes let out a breath and nodded. "I'm grateful that you'll let me come with you. In fact, I'm grateful to all of you. I know I don't say it enough and I don't show it, but I am. I'm going to find something I'm good at and prove my worth. Even if I don't find a bond, I need to have a purpose in life. Once I find that bond, I don't want to be a parasite. Who would want to mate to a demon who it would seem only needs the bond for life, not for anything else?"

Balin reached out and gripped Fawkes' shoulder with his free hand. "You'll find your place and when you do, we'll be by your side."

With that they cut the cake, drank, ate, and enjoyed the party that his friends had thrown for him. He needed to get out of his pity parties and get over himself.

After he said his goodbyes, he went back to the triad's home and picked up his duffle bag. He'd come to their home with nothing but the pants and boots he wore, but had at least collected a few clothes and belongings in the process.

Jamie hugged him hard, but he pulled away, knowing he needed to let the triad find their way as new parents without him. It was odd that he was going to another home with a new baby in the midst, but at least he knew how to change diapers now.

He shuddered at the thought but went to Hunter's side in the backyard anyway. Babies wouldn't scare him away, damn it.

Well, maybe.

"Ready?" Hunter asked.

"Yep. Thank you for this."

"It's no worries. You'll be staying in the guest house behind ours. I would have given you the guest room, but Leslie is staying there."

"Leslie?" Fawkes asked. "She's Dorian's sister right?" He'd heard about the male wolf who had almost killed Becca and Hunter and vaguely remembered the submissive sister who was on his friends' side of the almost-war.

Hunter nodded, a shadow passing over his eyes before he blinked them away. "She's a good girl." He let out a snort then shook his head. "I say girl, but she's only twenty years younger than me."

Fawkes frowned. "So that would make her around forty then. Still pretty young in the scheme of things."

Hunter raised a brow. "Still older than you."

"Most people are in our line of work."

"Okay, let's get to the den. Since the den is still in the human realm, we're not going to open a portal like most people do. It's more of a gateway to reach beyond our shields. Our den, like most, is located deep within a forest. You can usually make it there by foot, but there's no point in doing so when we can open the gateway."

Fawkes nodded, letting all the knowledge he could gleam seep in. He wanted to know all about the realms that he could. Since he wouldn't be returning to hell anytime soon, knowing everything he could about all others couldn't hurt.

Hunter opened the gateway and Fawkes stepped through. Rather than the normal fire and brimstone portal he was used to, this was almost a breath of fresh air. Soon he found himself standing amongst the trees, the scent of wolf and Pack filling his nostrils.

Becca, who had come back to the den earlier to put Hazel to bed, stood in the doorway of their home and waved.

"Good to see you, Fawkes," she called. "Hunter will show you where you're sleeping and in the morning, come right on in and we'll have breakfast and show you around."

"Thanks, Becca."

Hunter stalked toward his mate, that single-focused determination making Fawkes uncomfortable. "Go to sleep, my mate. I will be in to tuck you in soon."

Fawkes turned away as Becca blushed. Thank the gods he was staying in a different home. The two lovebirds were still newlyweds, despite having a new baby around. They'd need time for each other.

That thought reminded him that Leslie was living with them. He wondered how uncomfortable it was for her to stay there.

"They're always like that," a soft voice said from his side and he turned, alarmed that he hadn't sensed another presence around him. It was as if his demon was comfortable around this stranger.

The voice came from pretty girl to his side. She had big brown eyes and straight long brown hair. On others, the combination of all browns might have been boring or plain, but Fawkes thought she looked beautiful.

She was tiny—at least a foot shorter than his six-foot-one frame. She looked like she could fit right under his arms against his side as he fought the world for her.

He blinked at that thought.

What the hell did that mean?

"Uh, you must be Leslie," he said, his voice oddly hoarse.

She smiled and it lit up her whole face. Gods, she was beautiful.

He'd never reacted to a woman like this. He sure as hell wasn't a virgin, he knew women, but this quiet woman with her downcast eyes made him feel like a tongue tied idiot.

"Yes, I'm Leslie. You must be Fawkes, the demon Hunter said

would be staying in the guest house."

Fawkes swallowed hard, not knowing what to say, what to do. He rubbed his palms against his thighs, wiping off the sweat that seemed to pour from him.

Hell, he needed to get a grip on whatever the fuck was going on with him.

"Yeah, that's me. You're staying in the main house, right?"

"For now. I think though that I'll be moving out soon."

Why? Did she have a mate? That would be horrible.

Wait. Why did he care? He didn't even know her.

"Why?"

Leslie gave a small smile. "With Hazel here, the house is a bit crowded. Well, there's tons of room physically, but the couple needs some time to breathe, you know? They've never really had the space since they've been mated. I've always been there."

Fawkes frowned. "Hunter doesn't seem like the type to do something he doesn't want to do. If he didn't want you there, he'd tell you."

Leslie snorted. "Sure he would, but he's also a dominant wolf who can't help himself. His wolf actually *knows* how to act around a submissive, meaning he needs to take care of me, even if his human half would rather have time alone with his mate."

Fawkes didn't quite understand what it meant to be a submissive wolf, but he wasn't about to go out and ask her.

He'd just ask Hunter later.

"I feel like I'm intruding too."

Leslie shrugged. "It sounds like you need it though."

Fawkes looked at her strangely. "What do you mean?"

"Hunter said you were in your transition, right?" He nodded. "That means you need to be around people you trust to make sure you have a support system. You won't be yourself until the year is over unless you find your mate first. The fact that Hunter would allow you to be here with his mate and child present tells you how much you mean to his family, Fawkes."

He blinked as shame wove through him. "I'd never hurt Becca or Hazel."

She nodded. "I know. Hunter trusts you."

He swallowed hard. "Do you?"

Her eyes widened then she looked around as if she were suddenly aware she was alone in the forest with a demon who was straddling the line between good and evil.

"I don't know you."

"Will you?"

"Will I what?"

"Will you get to know me?"

"If we're living so near each other, I suppose we will. I don't think that's what you're asking though." She bit her lip and lowered her eyes, a pretty blush covering her skin.

"I don't think that's what I'm asking either."

"I'm going to go in and let Hunter know you're ready to see your new home." She took a step away from him and he fought the urge to move closer so he could feel her skin.

He wanted to know if she was as soft as she looked.

He wanted to rub himself against her so all other males would be able to smell his scent on her and know she was his.

He froze.

Oh shit.

She blinked hard as if she'd heard his thoughts. "I'll see you tomorrow, Fawkes."

She turned and ran as if she were being chased.

Well hell.

That wasn't the best way to meet the woman who could be his true half.

His mate.

His savior.

What the hell was he going to do now?

"Fawkes?" Hunter called, interrupting his thoughts.

"Yeah?" He shook his head, clearing his thoughts. "Sorry, what?"

Hunter followed his gaze to where Leslie had raced off to and frowned. "Be careful with her, Fawkes. She's been through a lot. Plus she's a submissive wolf who's trying to find her way."

"What does being submissive mean?" He needed to know and

this seemed like the best time to
ask.

"It means her wolf needs to
be taken cared for by a dominant.
It's not that she's a doormat, far
from it. Because of wolves like
hers, other wolves are able to
have the strength they need to
fight for the Pack. Without them,
well, I wouldn't want to think
what our Pack would look like.
Right now though, the Pack isn't
healthy. We're working on it, but
it's taking time. Not all the
dominants know how to treat
submissives. Leslie needs space
from people who treat her wrong.
She needs to find her footing."

Well if that wasn't a warning
to stay away from her, Fawkes
didn't know what was. His demon
wanted her but he didn't have his
own footing yet, let alone step out
of his zone and hurt another.

He gave Hunter a nod but didn't let his gaze stray from where Leslie had stood.

He'd give her time to find herself then he'd follow her. He'd made his choice and for some reason he had a feeling Leslie would be the one to help him keep it made.

CHAPTER FOUR

Why couldn't she just get the nerve to *ask* him what he felt? Leslie wondered to herself. It had been two months since she met the demon who made her wolf beg for more and prance around like a show-pup yet she hadn't made a move.

Neither had he.

Could her wolf be wrong?

Maybe Fawkes wasn't her true half and mate.

That thought seemed to depress her.

Fawkes had moved into the guest house and immediately entwined himself within the Pack. Liam and Alec loved him—training with the demon daily with not only normal fighting but with swords as well. Hunter would join them and the four of them, along with a few others who came to watch or play, would train for hours.

Fawkes would then walk around the den, learning what he could about how a Pack worked. He learned how the maternal females were stronger than most dominant males. They had to be considering they were the ones that raised the pups into who they would grow up to be.

The maternal females loved him. Apparently they loved his

smile and the way he would let
the pups climb up his body—sans
claws since they were taught at a
young age not to use them while
in wolf form. He wrestle with the
pups on the ground, treating
them as if they were his own and
precious.

While in the main house he'd
walk around holding Hazel to his
chest, singing in a low—and
damn sexy—baritone. The little
girl was in love with him already
and she knew Becca trusted him
with her heart.

After all, the fiery leprechaun
trusted him with her child and
mate.

If only Leslie could work up
the nerves to make a move.

When she'd seen him behind
the house that first night her wolf
had howled, pacing around and
trying to get out to touch him.
Gods, she wanted to feel his

hands in her fur...and tangled in her hair.

She might not be a virgin, but it had been *way* too long since she'd had any form of contact that wasn't brotherly...or creepy as hell.

Colin and his crew still bothered her but they had seemed to step back a bit since Liam, Alec, and Hunter had warned them off.

She knew it wouldn't last though.

It never did.

If only that were the worst of her problems though.

Her wolf—and her human half—wanted Fawkes.

Badly.

If only she knew how to make that clear. She knew other species mated with wolves as she'd seen firsthand evidence of it with Becca and Hunter. So that meant that the demon who was

currently wrestling with his
choice to be good *could* be her
true half.

She just had to ask him.

She let out a snort.

Sure like that was easy.

"What's so funny?" Fawkes
asked as he walked to her side.
He came up right beside her but
didn't touch her.

Her wolf whimpered at the
lack of contact and it took all in
her power not to lean closer and
rub herself along his body,
scenting him so no other female
would dare come near him.

Oh, she'd seen the other
females watch him. There might
not be as many females as males
in the Pack, but those who were
there and mateless watched her
demon.

Yes, *hers*.

She just had to make it that
way.

"Leslie?" He reached out as if he were going to cup her face, then fisted his hand before lowering his arm to his side.

Her wolf whimpered and she wanted to scream. Why couldn't she make the first move? Damn being submissive.

"What? Oh, nothing's funny. I was just thinking."

He searched her face and she stared into those black eyes with flecks of red. Since they were within the den, he didn't wear contacts. None of them did. Once any of them left the den, they wore contacts to protect their secret. Though Leslie's eyes were more brown than gold or yellow because she wasn't as dominate as Hunter and the like, she still wore them in public. She never knew if something were to anger her wolf or cause her to want to shift.

It had never happened before, but she wasn't about to take the chance.

"Why are you so nervous around me?" Fawkes asked. "Do I scare you in some way? I promise I won't hurt you or change my mind about the choice I made."

She shook her head. "I'm not afraid you'll hurt me." Well, that wasn't quite true. She was terrified he didn't think she was his true half and she'd end up alone forever.

Wow. Dramatic much?

"Then why do you keep to yourself?"

"I thought you were the one doing it. You've stayed away since that first night we met, barely saying one word to me."

"I...I thought because you were submissive that I had to be careful around you."

She blinked, hurt arching through her body like a painful caress. "What?"

"Hunter said you need time so I was staying away so I wouldn't make you nervous."

The hurt intensified, but this time laced with anger. "He said what?"

"He said you'd been hurt so I stayed away, making sure I didn't do anything to scare you. I know I'm new to the Pack, so I didn't want to invade your territory."

"You think that because I'm a submissive wolf that I need to be held with kids' gloves or something?"

"No, I mean, I don't know. No one will tell me how to act around you," he blurted then shut his eyes. "Hell, now I sound like an idiot. I swear I know how to talk around people but you make me nervous."

All at once that hurt and anger went away, something much warmer replacing it. "You make me nervous to but not in a bad way," she added on at the end as something like pain crossed his features.

"How do I make you nervous?" he asked.

She took a deep breath and took the plunge. "You feel it don't you? That connection?" Her wolf pranced around, beyond joyed that she'd finally voiced their feelings—or at least started to.

Fawkes smiled and her wolf fell in love. Leslie, however, was a bit slower. She barely knew the demon—something she'd have to change soon. It wasn't as if the human part of her would fall in love at first sight.

Okay, maybe lust at first sight, but that was a whole other matter.

He reached out and cupped her cheek and she froze before leaning into his touch—his *first* touch. He smelled of fire and brimstone, but with that scent of man that could be hers. Her nipples pebbled and her stomach clenched.

"How about we start over?" he asked and she nodded, his calloused fingertips brushing against her face.

"I'd love that though I might have to kick Hunter for making you think you had to stay away from me."

Fawkes grinned. "Well, Leslie, it's nice to meet you. I'm Fawkes, a demon who's about to get a little testy because I'm not taking souls."

She nodded knowing what he was doing was harder than anything she'd ever faced—even her brother.

"I'm Leslie, a submissive wolf who's trying to figure out what to do next."

"What do you want to do next?"

"Find my own way," she said honestly, surprised she'd even voiced that thought at all.

He pulled his hand away and before she could feel the loss he ran his palm down her arm, then tangled their fingers together.

"How are you going to do that?" he asked, looking genuinely interested.

"I haven't the first clue." She laughed as she said it and Fawkes smiled.

"Well, okay then. I'm sort of on the same path. I haven't the faintest idea what I'm going to do with the rest of my life. I mean, I spent the first part of it thinking I'd be a warrior demon and follow my father's footsteps."

"Your father being Lucifer." She'd heard the rumors around the Pack that he was the son of the Devil. While most people had taken to Fawkes easily, others were still weary. After all, it wasn't every day they met the son of the demon humans and Pack alike feared like no other.

"Does that bother you?"

"No," she answered honestly. "You're not your father, the same as I'm not my brother." That was something she knew for sure. She might have had the same blood running through her veins as Dorian, but she wasn't the traitor he'd been. She wasn't evil. Fawkes wasn't evil either. He'd chosen to go against his realm, knowing he'd die because of it to choose good.

That was something the Devil could never say.

"I could kill Dorian all over again for what he did to you and the Pack."

"I take it you've heard it all."

Fawkes nodded, running his thumb over her knuckle. She held back a shiver at the touch. They might not be talking about what was going on between the two of them, but at least they were talking at all.

"I know how Dorian and others in the council tried to take over the Pack. They betrayed Hunter and sent him to hell. That's how I met Hunter."

"I know." He'd saved Hunter and a few of Becca's friends.

"The council wanted to rule the Pack like a democracy, rather than with the Alpha. I'm not completely sure, but I think that wolves *need* their Alpha. Right?"

"Totally. We're not human. We need the Alpha to keep our wolves in line and remind us we're not alone. That's why becoming a lone wolf is so hard—wolves need that bond with the Pack. Trying to rule by council makes no sense to us and it shouldn't. Most of the council—besides Alec and Liam—were idiots anyway. They just wanted the power for themselves and didn't really care about the good of the Pack. A good Alpha and Beta care for the Pack as much as they lead it if not more."

"I'm glad Dorian failed, even if it took too long to take him down."

She remembered the beatings and when he'd tried to sell her for the good of his plan but pushed those memories to the side. She was stronger now.

"I'm sorry for bringing that up," Fawkes sighed. "I hate that I put that sadness on your face."

Leslie shook her head. "You didn't. Dorian did, but I'm getting better."

"I know. You're stronger than you think you are. I kept away, not talking about what my demon feels, because Hunter said you were submissive and needed time, but I think I did the wrong thing. You're not weak and frail, you're the glue and support of the Pack. I should have seen that."

Leslie's eyes widened at that. "You thought I was weak and frail?"

"Hell no," Fawkes grumbled. "That was the problem. I thought that's what I was supposed to see but I didn't. All I saw was a woman looking for who she was. A woman I wanted to get to know."

"I stay at Hunter and Becca's because I can't keep away from Hazel," she said, ignoring the last part of his statement for now. "I know Becca can handle her child on her own, but I'm weak when it comes to babies."

Fawkes smiled. "You want one of your own?"

"So badly but I want a mate first." She blushed at that and Fawkes squeezed her hand.

"You're my true half, Leslie, aren't you?"

She started at his words, surprised he'd be so blatant, but happy he was.

"Yes, I think so."

Fawkes swallowed hard and she watched the way his throat worked. "You know, I planned on visiting all the realms I could, praying I'd find my true half and yet here you are."

"I don't know you, Fawkes."

"I don't know you either, Leslie, but I want to get to know you. I'm not saying we should mate and just go full steam ahead, but I'd like to I don't know...court you?"

She held back a laugh at that term. "Court?"

He blushed a sweet shade and shrugged. "I don't know. I'm not any good at this. You'd think I'd have prepared something after staring at you for two months but you make me lose what I'm going to say."

"I know exactly how you feel."

"So we take things slow? We learn each other while we learn ourselves? I don't think either of us is ready to jump ahead and listen to fate, but I don't want to lose something important either."

Relief filled her. "Oh, thank the gods," she laughed. "I still want to find out who I am and I know you're the same, but if we can find out together? I'm totally okay with that."

"I know you're a wolf and strong, but I also want you to know that I'll protect you. Okay? I know women nowadays are vocal about their independence but my demon needs to let you know that I'll be your warrior."

She blushed at that thought. "Okay, but you need to help me learn to kick ass too."

Fawkes threw his head back and laughed. "Deal. I'm going to kiss you now. Okay?"

She nodded, suddenly shy.

He ran his hands up her arms, over her shoulders, then cupped her face. Her breaths came in pants as she waited. His dark eyes lit with red then he lowered his lips.

She closed her eyes at the first touch of his lips against hers. His touch was gentle, soft, as if he were afraid to spook her. Then his tongue darted out to lick the seam of her lips. She opened for him immediately, letting his tongue brush along hers. She gasped at his taste—a subtle musk that was all Fawkes combined with the sweet tea he'd had with lunch.

He rubbed his thumbs along her cheeks as he deepened the kiss, his tongue delving deeper as he gained confidence.

She moaned into him, her body going flush against his as he pulled away slightly to kiss the corners of her mouth before going back to a deeper kiss.

Her mind went blank as she let Fawkes take control. Her wolf knew he'd never go too far, never push her where she didn't want to go. That was what made her a submissive. Her wolf trusted the dominant who held her with such reverence, the woman part of her let go and let it happen.

She wouldn't do this for anyone else.

Hadn't done it for anyone else.

This was her true half, the man and demon she'd learn more about.

Finally he pulled away, their breaths panting in synch. Leslie swallowed hard and he did the same. He smiled at her and she knew everything would be all right. It didn't make any sense as to why, but she'd trust fate on this one.

She had to.

"You're fucking kidding me," Colin spat from their sides.

Fawkes pulled her behind him and growled—a different growl from a wolf, but a growl nonetheless.

"Hiding behind this little demon, you bitch?"

Fawkes moved forward and Leslie gripped his arm, pulling him back. "No, don't. It's not worth it," she whispered.

Fawkes looked down at her, keeping one eye on Colin. "I'll tear him limb from limb. He's the one who's been hurting you, hasn't he?"

She didn't want Fawkes to fight. She was tired of fighting, tired of feeling scared of the stronger wolves. She just wanted to take him away and get to know him, not deal with what could happen.

"You think you can just come into our Pack and take our females?" Colin asked, his eyes going wolf.

Fawkes searched her face then sighed. It broke her heart that she was forcing him to do something against his nature, but she couldn't stand fighting, not after what she'd been through.

"You need to watch your step, Colin," Fawkes said, his voice laced with anger. "I'm not fighting you now because my mate wishes it, but stand aside."

Mate?

Oh no, he shouldn't have said that. Not yet.

Her wolf preened at the title, but she knew Colin wouldn't like it.

She wasn't disappointed.

"You think you can mate with one of ours, *demon*?"

"She's mine," Fawkes growled. "I'm not going to fight you. I'm not going to let you treat her like anything less than the proud wolf she is."

Colin looked over Leslie's head and she scented Liam and Alec coming up from behind them.

"Is there a problem here, boys?" Liam asked as he stood on one side, Alec on the other.

Colin curled a lip then spit on the ground in front of them. "No.

Not yet." He turned on his heel, his shoulders tense.

Leslie relaxed next to Fawkes and he wrapped his arm around her.

"You're going to have to tell me why I did that later," Fawkes whispered and she nodded.

"I don't know exactly what that was about, but you'll have to tell me later," Liam said before he walked away, Alec following quietly behind like always.

"Thank you," she whispered.

"I'd do anything for you, Leslie. You know that. It's what being a true half and mate means, but you'll have to tell me. Okay?"

She nodded then wrapped her arms around his waist. She'd forced a dominant demon to stand back and not fight. What kind of person did that make her?

She needed to make some decisions and quickly. If she didn't get over her aversion to fighting, she might lose the one thing she hadn't known she could have.

CHAPTER FIVE

She felt so soft and warm against his side that Fawkes wasn't sure if he wanted to let her go. Ever.

That might prove a problem considering they were in public and some of the other wolves were staring. Really, though, he should have been used to the staring by then. They always watched him, first with fear, then with trepidation. Now, it was a mix of curiosity and sheer bafflement.

He wanted to think it was merely because he was a demon with his arm wrapped around a wolf, but he had a feeling it had much more to do with Leslie herself, than him.

That was something he'd have to change.

He'd stayed away from her for two months because he'd been an idiot. At first it was because he wasn't exactly sure what he was feeling. After all, he'd never met his true half before. For all he knew the connection he felt was because she was absolutely gorgeous.

The last thing he wanted to do was follow her around like a helpless little demon because his dick got hard.

He frowned and shook off
that last crude thought. Leslie
was worth more than that.

Not that Colin and his little
crew had the same thought.

If Leslie hadn't held him back
the day before he'd have punched
that fucker's face in.

Colin, Ben and the other
wolves he hadn't cared to get
their names of before, seemed to
want to have their own small
Pack within the main Pack.
Hunter had told him that he had
the crew on his radar, but
technically, they showed more
dominant wolves respect.

The Beta of the Pack had
already threatened to kick their
asses and it hadn't been enough.
He'd given Fawkes—an outsider—
permission to provide justice. If
the crew came anywhere near
Leslie, he'd fight back.

Well, he would if Leslie would
let him. For some reason she had

an aversion to violence. No, he knew the reason.

Dorian.

That brother of hers had scared her more than the others thought. Sure, she stayed with Hunter at first because she'd had nowhere else to go, but then most of them had thought she stayed because she liked it. He'd seen the way she was around Hazel and how her eyes would light up every time she saw the little girl. She'd sigh with contentment when she held her and would laugh when Hunter would act overprotective.

Yet, Fawkes had a feeling she stayed for other reasons.

No, not because he was near, but because she didn't want to leave.

She *couldn't* leave.

Staying in a house with a sadistic, power-hungry, asshole had scarred her. He knew she shied away from violence, but she was a wolf.

How could she stay away from it all?

Wolves here entwined with the darkness and violence as much as demons were. Wolves went on monthly hunts that always led to blood or sex. That was just the way of it. He knew she was submissive, but now she was ignoring her call—ignoring who she was.

He didn't know what to do about it.

"Fawkes? What's wrong?"

He looked down into her big brown eyes, then kissed her nose. She sighed against him and he hugged her tighter.

"Nothing's wrong," he lied.

She wrinkled her nose and pulled back from him but still kept her arms wrapped around his waist. "You're lying."

"I'm just thinking," he said then leaned for another kiss. He couldn't get enough of her taste. He knew that sudden love-at-first sight thing wasn't quite accurate, it was more of a could-be-perfect-forever-and-ever-at-first sight thing, but he didn't care.

His demon wanted this wolf. Badly.

"Okay, fine, but I want to know later."

He nodded, knowing he'd have to get her to talk about why she'd wanted him to stand back and let Colin growl without getting his face kicked in.

They stood to the side of the den circle, the trees swaying behind them in the breeze. There was going to be a dominance battle within the circle a bit later and Fawkes wanted to watch as he'd never seen one before. He had a feeling Leslie would want to leave, but she wouldn't be able to.

All wolves would have to be present—especially since she lived with the Beta.

It would be bad form to miss it and show weakness if she were too scared to show up.

He'd stand by her side though. No matter what.

"Tell me more about you," she whispered.

There were others around them, but they were off to the side enough that they had a semblance of privacy.

They'd already talked about growing up without mothers and her case, without a father. Dorian had raised her—something she hadn't wanted to get into. He'd already gone into detail on how he'd met Hunter and Ambrose and how Balin had trained him had a young age.

"Well, I'm the youngest son in my family," he began.

"Do you have any sisters?" she asked as she played with his fingers. Her hands were so small compared to his.

Not weak, but fragile none the less. If he'd been a wolf, he'd probably already have gone to his animal side and marked her. Because he was a demon, he wouldn't do that, but the idea of her bearing his mark held a certain appeal. That way everyone would know she was his and when she marked him, the same would be true of he being hers.

"No, I don't have any sisters," Fawkes answered as he trailed his fingers up her arm, loving the way her body shuddered.

"That's odd considering how old Lucifer is," Leslie commented. She ran her other hand up his stomach, seemingly unaware they were in public and all he wanted to do was bend her over and mount her.

Well, he'd make it less crude, but still.

"Either my dad is really, really good at making boys, or any demons who have his baby girls hide them," Fawkes answered. "I don't think Lucifer would want to acknowledge girls anyway. He's a misogynist ass that way. So, yeah, I guess I could have some sisters out there, but none that call me brother. Technically, I don't really know what it feels like to have siblings. I wasn't raised with the rest of them."

Leslie furrowed her brow and he leaned down to kiss it. She sighed against him then pulled back to look into his eyes.

"I kind of wish I hadn't been raised with my sibling."

He nodded, waiting for her to continue. They'd said they'd take this whole true half thing slow so they could get to know one another. This was one thing he'd been waiting for.

"He ruined everything, Fawkes. He might have beaten me, but the physical things don't matter as much as everything else." She looked over her shoulder and he squeezed her side before moving her toward the trees. Here at least people wouldn't be likely to overhear.

Though he wanted to comment on the beating part of her statement, he stayed quiet, knowing she needed to talk.

"I'm afraid, Fawkes. I *hate* being afraid. What kind of wolf does that make me? I'm afraid of others fighting. I'm afraid of wanting to fight myself. I'm *supposed* to want to fight for my Pack, even as a submissive, but I can't."

He swallowed hard and slid his hand through her hair. She

leaned into his touch and his demon calmed.

"I don't know, Leslie. I don't know how to fix this. All I can do is promise that I'll be by your side. I know Hunter and Becca feel the same way, well not the *same* way as me, but they think of you as family. Liam and Alec too."

"I don't think I can be fixed, Fawkes."

Not knowing what to do, he leaned down and kissed her.

Hard.

She sucked in a breath then sank into the kiss. He wrapped his arms around her and pulled her up so her feet dangled. She wrapped her arms around his neck and he deepened the kiss.

When he pulled back they were both out of breath but she smiled. "Okay, that might help."

He snorted, but let her down to the ground. "Come on, the dominance battle is starting."

She nodded, but he saw the tension that had left her when he kissed her slide right back into her body.

Damn.

As they walked toward the circle again Fawkes held back a curse. Colin stood in the center, shirtless and wearing a sneer.

"Who is it you wish to fight?" Hunter asked, anger laced within his tone.

"As my right as a dominant wolf, I claim a battle with the newest member of our Pack, Fawkes."

Fawkes stiffened and Leslie gasped.

What the fuck?

Murmurs and shouts echoed around the circle while the Beta raised his hand to quiet them all. They immediately shut up.

"Fawkes is but a guest, not Pack," Hunter stated.

His words didn't hurt Fawkes. It was true. To others because called out as non-Pack might have hurt, but Fawkes wasn't a wolf.

"He's staying at the home of the Beta and putting his hands on a woman that I desire to claim as my own. That gives me the right." Colin folded his arms over his chest and smirked again.

Fawkes risked a glance at Hunter. The Beta looked ready to tear Colin limb from limb—something Fawkes would gladly help with.

This fight for dominance was a joke. He'd learned enough about the Pack during his small time there that Colin couldn't outright ask for a battle like this, but he could provoke an outsider in fighting.

If the outsider lost, then he'd be banned from the den.

Banned from Leslie.

That result was enough that he wouldn't have thought twice about fighting. He'd stand back and let Colin make an ass out of himself so he couldn't leave her. However, he knew that if he said no now, it would only be a matter of time before Colin tried again, albeit another approach.

Colin wanted Leslie because of her blood, not because of who she was. Fawkes wanted Leslie because of their fate *and* who she was. He loved the way she smiled, the way she helped people when they weren't looking, the way she slid to his side without even knowing it.

He'd fight Colin to the ends of the depths of hell for her.

Fighting though would drive Leslie away.

Did he really have a choice?

"I'll fight," Fawkes growled.

Leslie sucked in a breath and he looked down at the betrayal in her eyes. Damn it. She'd have to get used to him fighting. He might not be down in hell, but he was still a warrior demon. He was stronger than Colin, but he had a feeling the other wolf didn't know that.

Good.

Risking her wrath, he pulled Leslie into his arms and kissed her hard.

"I'll win this. I promise. I know you hate fighting, but I'll win this and it'll be over."

She sighed and shook her head. "Will it, Fawkes? Will it be over?"

He walked into to circle, taking off his shirt as he did so. He wanted the freedom of movement. He let his horns grow from his head, the sight startling people be he didn't care.

He glanced at Hunter who gave him a small nod. "Colin, you've chosen to fight a demon.

He can't shift into wolf, so neither shall you."

Colin glared. "They why did he shift to his demon form?"

Because he was tired of hiding, but Fawkes didn't say that.

"Fawkes, does your demon form give you advantage?" Hunter asked. "Remember, I can smell a lie."

Fawkes wasn't sure Hunter could actually do that, but he'd let the wolf make the others think so. Anything to keep the Pack safe.

"No. My horns do nothing but remind me who I am."

With that Colin attacked.

Fawkes countered the punch and clawed back.

Colin screamed as Fawkes slid his claws into the wolf's side. "Yield."

Colin narrowed his eyes but shook his head.

Fawkes growled. "You'll never have her. She's mine. More importantly, she's her own. She gets the choice. She gets the decision. You get *nothing*. Don't make me kill you. I will, but I don't want to watch her deal with the bloodshed. You're nothing, Colin. Just a wolf who wanted something he couldn't have so decided to make it painful for all others. Yield."

Colin lowered his gaze and Fawkes slid his claws out of the other man.

Ben and the other wolves ran to Colin's side, defeat heavy on their scent.

"This battle is over," Hunter declared. "Fawkes is now Pack."

Fawkes blinked. He hadn't known defeating the wolf would lead to this. He risked a glance at Leslie who had tears running down her cheeks but she didn't run away from the blood on his hands.

He lowered his head to his Alpha and Beta then walked to Leslie's side.

"Forgive me," he rasped.

She looked into his eyes and nodded. "I forgive you for what you had to do. I know you had no choice, but I don't know if I can deal with the violence, Fawkes. Help me."

He wanted to hold her, pull her closer and never let her go, but he didn't want to get blood on her. She seemed to understand his dilemma and gripped his hands.

"What's wrong with me, Fawkes?"

He leaned down and captured her lips. "Nothing is wrong, baby. Nothing."

"Then why don't I like violence?"

"Because you'd rather deal with others with words, rather than fists. Can you deal with what I am? I'm a warrior, Leslie. I can't help it."

She nodded. "For you? Yes. I'll deal. You'll have to help me. I hate who I've become."

He kissed her again then pulled back. "I love who you are, Leslie. You have a good heart. Just because you're a wolf, doesn't mean you have to love bloodshed. Remember that. You never have to fight. I'll be the one to fight for you. You just have to be by my side to make sure I'm okay."

She smiled then widened her eyes as she pushed him out of the way. Surprised she'd done that, he let her move him then turned as she growled, her claws out.

She shifted to a wolf in a flash of light, the beauty of it leaving him breathless. Colin had also changed to a wolf, trying to pounce on them. As a submissive, Leslie shouldn't have been able to fight back, but then again, someone had threatened her mate.

The two wolves hit hard, a whimper escaping from Leslie. She was at least half the size as Colin and weaker. It didn't matter how skilled she might have been, it would be a losing battle.

She tried to bite Colin but he pinned her to the ground. Fawkes screamed then wrapped his claws around Colin's neck and squeezed. The other wolf let out a strangled gasp then went limp.

He'd broken the bastard's neck in one move.

He threw the wolf to the side then pulled Leslie—still in wolf form—in his arms. She shifted back to her human from and he found his arms full of a very naked Leslie.

"Baby, are you okay?" He ran his hands down her body, checking for any injury. She kissed his jaw and settled into his arms. He was aware of others surrounding them, outrage and disbelief in their voices, but he ignored them.

"I'm fine. I didn't want him to hurt you."

"Goddess, you scared me." He kissed her hard then pulled her into his arms as tight as he could, trying to shield her nudity from the others.

"I fought him, Fawkes. I didn't back down."

The pride in her voice made him want to weep. "Yes, baby. You did amazing but never do that again. You about killed me."

She smiled up at him and he lost his breath. "I promise to let you fight on your own from now on. Maybe."

He rolled his eyes. "We're going to talk about this later," he whispered and she nodded against him.

She was stronger than she thought she'd been, but he knew they had more to work on.

CHAPTER SIX

Leslie sat in Hunter's guest house and watched Fawkes stalk toward her, clean and fresh from the shower. His hair touched his shoulders, way too sexy for his own good.

Since she'd first met him, she'd known that he was damn attractive and way too perfect for her wolf.

It had taken awhile for her to realize he was perfect for the human part of her too.

"We need to talk about what happened, Les," he whispered as he rocked from one foot to another. He looked as uncomfortable as she'd felt before she realized that she'd only been kidding herself.

For far too long.

Gods, she hurt him. She'd forced him to change who he was—even for a little bit—because she was so afraid.

"I'm sorry."

His chin rose so fast she was afraid he'd have neck damage. "What? What do you have to be sorry for?"

"I held back because I was afraid."

He sat next to her on the couch and pulled her in his arms, his scent wrapping around her like a worn blanket.

"You had reasons to hold back, baby."

"Did I?" She shook her head. "No, I was an idiot. I held back not because I wanted to get to know you, well, okay, I *did* want to know you better before we bonded, but that wasn't the whole reason. I knew you were a warrior from what Hunter had told me about you and just by looking at you that first night."

Fawkes nodded. "And that scared you."

"Yes. I hate that it did. I pushed you away, or at least I *stayed* away from you at first because I hadn't been sure I could take it. I wasn't afraid you'd hurt me, not really."

He kissed her temple, a shudder running through his body. "I'd never hurt you, Les."

"I know. I *know*. It was more of what would happen if I let my wolf out."

She wanted to kiss the frown right off his face. "What do you mean?"

"Dorian and I share the same blood, Fawkes." She held up her hand when he opened his mouth to speak. "No, let me finish my crazy thoughts. I thought that if I gave into the violence that's inherent in the Pack, I'd become him. I know it makes no sense, but I didn't want to be that wolf."

Fawkes cupped her face, his eyes so full of sympathy and...love that she just wanted to wrap herself around him and never let go.

Soon.

"You could never become that, Leslie. You fought today to protect someone you care about. You stood by and watched me kill a man today to protect you. Don't you see? You're stronger than you thought."

She smiled at him then kissed his jaw, loving the way the bristles on his chin felt against her lips. "I know that now. I'm a wolf. I need to get over my fears and I will. At least I will with your help."

Fawkes nodded. "I will. You know I will. Leslie, you mean everything to me. I came out of hell not knowing what I would do, what choice I would make, but there really wasn't a choice for me. I don't want to live my life without the other half of my soul. I want to be with you until the end of the earth. I want to grow with you, watch you grow round with our children, and watch you become the wolf you've always wanted to be."

Love and warmth filled her chest and she threw her arms around his neck. "I love you, Fawkes."

He kissed the side of her neck, sending delicious shivers down her body. "I love you too, my Leslie. Gods, I love you so much."

"I want to bond, Fawkes. I don't want to wait."

He pulled back and cupped her face. "Are you sure? Right now? I want to make sure when we bond that you know it's because I want you and you want me, not so you can save me from my demonic self."

She shook her head, then kissed the center of his palm. "I want you to not have to worry about that, yes, but I want to feel you in here." She placed her own palm over her heart. "I want that bond more than anything, Fawkes."

He smiled, his face growing even more handsome than when he brooded. "Anything, love. Anything."

He cupped her face then lowered his lips. Gods, he tasted amazing, like hell's heat just cooled down for her mixed with mint. She breathed into him, letting him take control. He ran his hands through her hair, tugging slightly, sending an unknown thrill down her spine.

He pulled back, his black eyes dancing with red flecks. "You liked that, didn't you?"

She licked her lips, loving the way his gaze followed the wet trail. "I like anything you do."

He grinned, this time not in humor, but in a feral need that almost made her come on the spot. "Good."

Whereas before his kisses were soft, tentative, these new ones where hard, demanding.

She loved it.

His lips nibbled along her jaw. He tugged her hair to the side, forcing her to arch her neck so he could lick and bite. She pussy clenched at that feeling of his teeth scraping along the juncture where her neck met her shoulder and she wiggled in his hold, needing to find release.

He bit down harder but didn't break the skin.

"I'll mark you tonight, baby, but not until we're both panting with so much need we'll combust."

Was it wrong she was about to combust right there?

He slowly slid his hands down her sides then up her shirt. The heat of his skin shocking against hers.

Though he'd let his demon side and horns show during the fight, he'd hid them again in the shower. For some reason she missed them.

"Didn't I hear something about demon horns

being...sensitive?" she asked then bit her lip.

Fawkes sucked in a breath and nodded. "Next time. If you touch my horns I'll blow right now and then we'll miss out on me sinking into that pussy of yours."

Okay, so apparently she *was* able to almost come by just his words.

Good to know.

He slowly slid up her shirt, leaving her in her bra and jeans. His eyes darkened, though the red specks seemed to glow.

"Gods, you're beautiful."

"Hurry, Fawkes. I'm burning up." She blushed at the admission and her demon licked her shoulders then cupped her breasts through her bra. Her nipples tightened to sharp points against his palms and she rocked against him.

"When you blush, you blush all over. It's sexy as hell."

"Fawkes..."

He didn't let her finish her moan, though she wasn't quite sure what she would have said short of begging.

He rolled her nipples between his fingers and pinched down through her bra. Hard.

She arched her back, pressing her breasts into his palms more. He quickly undid the front clasp of her bra, letting her breasts fall in his palms.

Heavy.

Ready.

He lowered his head, pulling her nipple between his teeth. She gasped as he flicked his tongue, causing her stomach to tighten, her pussy doing the same.

When she was wiggling in his hold, he lavished her other breast, forcing her to rock against him, begging for release.

He chuckled against her skin, the rasp another form of torture.

Finally, he lowered himself so he knelt on the floor in front of the couch and moved so he was between her legs.

She swallowed hard, silent but her heavy pants as he undid her jeans and slid them, along with her panties down her legs. He threw them to the side and she found herself naked on the couch while he knelt fully clothed between her legs.

"What are you doing?" she asked, hoping he was about to do what she thought he was. She might have been a submissive wolf, but she wanted his mouth on her.

Now.

"I'm going to taste this sweet cunt of yours then fuck you with my fingers until you come around me. Then I'm going to take you to the bedroom and fuck you with my cock until both of us are boneless, marked, mated, and whole."

She blinked, holding herself back from coming from his words alone.

"Okay."

He grinned again then lowered his face to her mound. He kissed the short hair she'd trimmed there then licked along her nether lips. He took this thumb and forefinger to spread her then sat back on his haunches and stared.

She would have been embarrassed if not for the hungry look on his face.

Before she could beg for his touch, he licked her clit, then sucked. She rocked her face against him, holding the couch so she didn't force him even closer. He sucked, licked, and nibbled along her clit and pussy until she radiated with need. A storm of heat and need tumbled within her and she felt the orgasm spark until it rolled over her, her body thrashing as she called his name. She threw back her head, closed her eyes, and rode the wave of pleasure her mate provided.

He continued to go down on her as she came off her high, her body drugged with pleasure. Then he licked up her body, until his lips found her own. She could taste herself on him and just thought it was about the hottest thing ever.

She felt his hands on her ass and suddenly she was in his arms, her legs wrapped around his waist, her wet heat against the thick line of his erection within the confines of his jeans.

"Bedroom?" he moaned.

She nodded and leaned to kiss up his neck as he walked them to his bedroom. He gently placed her on the bed and she leaned back on her arms as he pulled off his shirt and pants.

"You weren't wearing underwear?" she asked, her stomach tightening again as she watched him.

He was gorgeous. Long and lean muscles covered his body. The ridges of his abdomen begged for her tongue and she couldn't wait to taste him.

Speaking of tasting...

She gulped as she studied his cock. Thick, long, and curved so it bounced on his stomach as he leaned over to kick the rest of his clothes out of the way.

"If you keep staring at me like that, things are going to end a bit quicker than I'd planned."

She smiled then stood quickly, pushing him on his back on the bed before he had a chance to understand what she planned.

"Leslie? Oh shit."

She cupped his balls and sucked the head of his cock into her mouth. She ran her tongue around the tip then along the little slit, loving the way his musky taste settled on his tongue.

"Leslie, if you do this, I'll come in your mouth when I really want to come in your pussy."

She pulled back, releasing his cock with a pop. "You're a demon. You can go again," she teased.

He groaned and tangled his hand in her hair, directing her where he wanted. She stroked up and down his length with one hand while rolling his balls in the palm of her other hand. She licked and sucked the sides of his cock then finally let him down her throat. The tip brushed the back of her throat and she relaxcd, letting him sit there for a minute before hollowing her cheeks and moving her head back. She bobbed up and down, sucking in time with the movement of her hands.

He gripped her hair and forced her to stay still. She loved that he took control. Loved. It. She raised her eyes and sought his gaze as he fucked her mouth. His cock slid in and out of her lips and she loved the taste, loved putting the control in his hands.

Finally she felt the first spurt of his seed on her tongue and she quickly swallowed as he came in her mouth. She let each drop roll down her throat then pulled away to lick his cock clean.

"Fuck, Leslie, you're amazing."

She gave him a naughty grin then he moved quicker than she could blink. Suddenly, she found herself on her back and his cock deep in her pussy as he thrust within her in one stroke.

"Gods," she moaned.

Fawkes froze above her. The strain of waiting clear on his face fixed with worry. "Did I hurt you?"

She shook her head. "No, please please. I need you."

He nodded the rolled his hips back, then forward. Her pussy tightened around him every time he tried to leave her and he groaned. He fucked her hard and fast, everything she needed as he leaned over her. He pulled back slightly and gripped her thighs pushing them up to her chest so he could get a bigger angle.

"Touch yourself," he ordered.

She nodded, then let her hand travel down her stomach to her clit. She rubbed circles on her clit and felt herself let go.

"Come. Come, my Leslie."

She did as she was told and came harder than she had in the living room. Fawkes shifted so he was still in her, but she was on top.

"Ride me, baby."

She nodded then rode him hard, letting her hips do most of the movement. He ran his hands up her body then cupped her breasts.

"Fawkes, I can't wait anymore. Please," she begged. It was so much. So many emotions, feelings, touches. "I need your mark. Please."

He moved again, this time sitting so she sat on his lap. He never stopped thrusting, showing her how strong he really was. He moved his neck to the side and she went on instinct.

She let her fangs pierce his flesh and she felt the bond snap in place as he came with her.

He held her close and then she moved back so he could mark her as well. Wolves were the ones who needed to mark, to claim, but she wanted his mark just as much.

Soon she found herself lying beside her mate, their bodies slick with sweat and exhaustion.

"That...that was amazing," he panted.

"That was a mating," she corrected.

"Fuck yeah." He turned and pushed her hair away from her face. "Wanna do it again?"

She laughed and buried herself into his side. "Always."

"I'm never letting you go, my Leslie. This is it for me. You're my choice. That bond you feel? That's perfection. I love you so much."

Tears filled her eyes and she kissed his chest, feeling his heartbeat beneath her lips. "You're my choice, Fawkes. No matter what happens, you'll always be my choice."

Fate might have given them to each other, but they'd chosen their own path.

Together.

The End

Coming Next:

Tangled Innocence

A Note from Carrie Ann

Thank you so much for reading **HIS CHOICE**. I do hope if you liked this story, that you would please leave a review. Not only does a review spread the word to other readers, they let us authors know if you'd like to see more stories like this from us. I love hearing from readers and talking to them when I can. If you want to make sure you know what's coming next from me, you can sign up for my newsletter at www.CarrieAnnRyan.com; follow me on twitter at @CarrieAnnRyan, or like my Facebook page. I also have a Facebook Fan Club where we have trivia, chats, and other goodies. You guys are the reason I get to do what I do and I thank you.

Make sure you're signed up for my MAILING LIST so you can know when the next releases are available as well as find giveaways and FREE READS.

The Dante's Circle series is an ongoing series with many novels already out. I hope you get a chance to catch up!

Dante's Circle Series:
Book 1: Dust of My Wings
Book 2: Her Warriors' Three Wishes
Book 3: An Unlucky Moon
The Dante's Circle Box Set (Contains Books 1-3)
Book 3.5: His Choice
Book 4: Tangled Innocence
Book 5: Fierce Enchantment
Book 6: An Immortal's Song (Coming in 2016)

Want to keep up to date with the next Carrie Ann Ryan Release? Receive Text Alerts easily!
Text CARRIE to 24587

About Carrie Ann and her Books

New York Times and USA Today Bestselling Author Carrie Ann Ryan never thought she'd be a writer. Not really. No, she loved math and science and even went on to graduate school in chemistry. Yes, she read as a kid and devoured teen fiction and Harry Potter, but it wasn't until someone handed her a romance book in her late teens that she realized that there was something out there just for her. When another author suggested she use the voices in her head for good and not evil, The Redwood Pack and all her other stories were born.

Carrie Ann is a bestselling author of over twenty novels and novellas and has so much more on her mind (and on her spreadsheets *grins*) that she isn't planning on giving up her dream anytime soon.

www.CarrieAnnRyan.com

Redwood Pack Series:
Book 1: An Alpha's Path
Book 2: A Taste for a Mate
Book 3: Trinity Bound
Book 3.5: A Night Away
Book 4: Enforcer's Redemption
Book 4.5: Blurred Expectations
Book 4.7: Forgiveness
Book 5: Shattered Emotions
Book 6: Hidden Destiny
Book 6.5: A Beta's Haven
Book 7: Fighting Fate
Book 7.5 Loving the Omega
Book 7.7: The Hunted Heart
Book 8: Wicked Wolf

The Talon Pack (Following the Redwood Pack Series):
Book 1: Tattered Loyalties
Book 2: An Alpha's Choice
Book 3: Mated in Mist (Coming in 2016)

The Redwood Pack Volumes:
Redwood Pack Vol 1
Redwood Pack Vol 2
Redwood Pack Vol 3
Redwood Pack Vol 4
Redwood Pack Vol 5
Redwood Pack Vol 6

Montgomery Ink:
Book 0.5: Ink Inspired
Book 0.6: Ink Reunited
Book 1: Delicate Ink
Book 1.5 Forever Ink
Book 2: Tempting Boundaries
Book 3: Harder than Words
Book 4: Written in Ink (Coming Oct 2015)

The Branded Pack Series:
(Written with Alexandra Ivy)
Books 1 & 2: Stolen and Forgiven
Books 3 & 4: Abandoned and
Unseen (Coming Sept 2015)

Dante's Circle Series:
Book 1: Dust of My Wings
Book 2: Her Warriors' Three
Wishes
Book 3: An Unlucky Moon
The Dante's Circle Box Set
(Contains Books 1-3)
Book 3.5: His Choice
Book 4: Tangled Innocence
Book 5: Fierce Enchantment
Book 6: An Immortal's Song
(Coming in 2016)

Holiday, Montana Series:
Book 1: Charmed Spirits
Book 2: Santa's Executive
Book 3: Finding Abigail
The Holiday Montana Box Set
(Contains Books 1-3)
Book 4: Her Lucky Love

Book 5: Dreams of Ivory

Tempting Signs Series:
Finally Found You

Excerpt: Wicked Wolf

From New York Times Bestselling Author Carrie Ann Ryan's Redwood Pack Series

There were times to drool over a sexy wolf.

Sitting in the middle of a war room disguised as a board meeting was not one of those times.

Gina Jamenson did her best not to stare at the dark-haired, dark-eyed man across the room. The hint of ink peeking out from under his shirt made her want to pant. She *loved* ink and this wolf clearly had a lot of it. Her own wolf within nudged at her, a soft brush beneath her skin, but she ignored her. When her wolf whimpered, Gina promised herself that she'd go on a long run in the forest later. She didn't understand why her wolf was acting like this, but she'd deal with it when she was in a better place. She just couldn't let her wolf have control right then—even for a man such as the gorgeous specimen a mere ten feet from her.

Today was more important than the wants and feelings of a half wolf, half witch hybrid.

Today was the start of a new beginning.

At least that's what her dad had told her.

Considering her father was also the Alpha of the Redwood Pack, he would be in the know. She'd been adopted into the family when she'd been a young girl. A rogue wolf during the war had killed her parents, setting off a long line of events that had changed her life.

As it was, Gina wasn't quite sure how she'd ended up in the meeting between the two Packs, the Redwoods and the Talons. Sure, the Packs had met before over the past fifteen years of their treaty, but this meeting seemed different.

This one seemed more important somehow.

And they'd invited—more like *demanded*—Gina to attend.

At twenty-six, she knew she was the youngest wolf in the room by far. Most of the wolves were around her father's age, somewhere in the hundreds. The dark-eyed wolf might have been slightly younger than that, but only slightly if the power radiating off of him was any indication.

Wolves lived a long, long time. She'd heard stories of her

people living into their thousands, but she'd never met any of the wolves who had. The oldest wolf she'd met was a friend of the family, Emeline, who was over five hundred. That number boggled her mind even though she'd grown up knowing the things that went bump in the night were real.

Actually, she *was* one of the things that went bump in the night.

"Are we ready to begin?" Gideon, the Talon Alpha, asked, his voice low. It held that dangerous edge that spoke of power and authority.

Her wolf didn't react the way most wolves would, head and eyes down, shoulders dropped. Maybe if she'd been a weaker wolf, she'd have bowed to his power, but as it was, her wolf was firmly entrenched within the Redwoods. Plus, it wasn't as if

Gideon was *trying* to make her bow just then. No, those words had simply been spoken in his own voice.

Commanding without even trying.

Then again, he *was* an Alpha.

Kade, her father, looked around the room at each of his wolves and nodded. "Yes. It is time."

Their formality intrigued her. Yes, they were two Alphas who held a treaty and worked together in times of war, but she had thought they were also friends.

Maybe today was even more important than she'd realized.

Gideon released a sigh that spoke of years of angst and worries. She didn't know the history of the Talons as well as she probably should have, so she didn't know exactly why there was always an air of sadness and pain around the Alpha.

Maybe after this meeting, she'd be able to find out more.

Of course, in doing so, she'd have to *not* look at a certain wolf in the corner. His gaze was so intense she was sure he was studying her. She felt it down in her bones, like a fiery caress that promised something more.

Or maybe she was just going crazy and needed to find a wolf to scratch the itch.

She might not be looking for a mate, but she wouldn't say no to something else. Wolves were tactile creatures after all.

"Gina?"

She blinked at the sound of Kade's voice and turned to him.

She was the only one standing other than the two wolves in charge of security—her uncle Adam, the Enforcer, and the dark-eyed wolf.

Well, *that* was embarrassing.

She kept her head down and forced herself not to blush. From the heat on her neck, she was pretty sure she'd failed in the latter.

"Sorry," she mumbled then sat down next to another uncle, Jasper, the Beta of the Pack.

Although the Alphas had called this meeting, she wasn't sure what it would entail. Each Alpha had come with their Beta, a wolf in charge of security...and her father had decided to bring her.

Her being there didn't make much sense in the grand scheme of things since it put the power on the Redwoods' side, but she wasn't about to question authority in front of another Pack. That at least had been ingrained in her training.

"Let's get started then," Kade said after he gave her a nod. "Gideon? Do you want to begin?"

Gina held back a frown. They *were* acting more formal than usual, so that hadn't been her imagination. The Talons and the Redwoods had formed a treaty during the latter days of the war between the Redwoods and the Centrals. It wasn't as though these were two newly acquainted Alphas meeting for the first time. Though maybe when it came to Pack matters, Alphas couldn't truly be friends.

What a lonely way to live.

"It's been fifteen years since the end of the Central War, yet there hasn't been a single mating between the two Packs," Gideon said, shocking her.

Gina blinked. Really? That couldn't be right. She was sure there had to have been *some* cross-Pack mating.

Right?

"That means that regardless of the treaties we signed, we don't believe the moon goddess has seen fit to fully accept us as a unit," Kade put in.

"What do you mean?" she asked, then shut her mouth. She was the youngest wolf here and wasn't formally titled or ranked. She should *not* be speaking right now.

She felt the gaze of the dark-eyed wolf on her, but she didn't turn to look. Instead, she kept her head down in a show of respect to the Alphas.

"You can ask questions, Gina. It's okay," Kade said, the tone of his voice not changing, but, as his daughter, she heard the softer edge. "And what I mean is, mating comes from the moon goddess. Yes, we can find our own versions of mates by not bonding fully, but a true bond, a true potential mate, is chosen by the moon goddess. That's how it's always been in the past."

Gideon nodded. "There haven't been many matings within the Talons in general."

Gina sucked in a breath, and the Beta of the Talons, Mitchell, turned her way. "Yes," Mitchell said softly. "It's that bad. It could be that in this period of change within our own pack hierarchy, our members just haven't found mates yet, but that doesn't seem likely. There's something else going on."

Gina knew Gideon—as well as the rest of his brothers and cousins—had come into power at some point throughout the end of the Central War during a period of the Talon's own unrest, but she didn't know the full history. She wasn't even sure Kade or the rest of the Pack royalty did.

There were some things that were intensely private within a Pack that could not—and should not—be shared.

Jasper tapped his fingers along the table. As the Redwood Beta, it was his job to care for their needs and recognize hidden threats that the Enforcer and Alpha might not see. The fact that he was here told Gina that the Pack could be in trouble from something *within* the Pack, rather than an outside force that Adam, the Enforcer, would be able to see through his own bonds and power.

"Since Finn became the Heir to the Pack at such a young age, it has changed a few things on our side," Jasper said softly. Finn was her brother, Melanie and Kade's oldest biological child. "The younger generation will be gaining their powers and bonds to the goddess earlier than would otherwise be expected." Her uncle looked at her, and she kept silent. "That means the current Pack leaders will one day not have the bonds we have to our Pack now. But like most healthy Packs, that doesn't mean we're set aside. It only means we will be there to aid the new hierarchy while they learn their powers. That's how it's always been in our Pack, and in others, but it's been a very long time since it's happened to us."

"Gina will one day be the Enforcer," Adam said from behind her. "I don't know when, but it will be soon. The other kids aren't old enough yet to tell who will take on which role, but since Gina is in her twenties, the shifts are happening."

The room grew silent, with an odd sense of change settling over her skin like an electric blanket turned on too high.

She didn't speak. She'd known about her path, had dreamed the dreams from the moon goddess herself. But that didn't mean she wanted the

Talons to know all of this. It seemed...private somehow.

"What does this have to do with mating?" she asked, wanting to focus on something else.

Gideon gave her a look, and she lowered her eyes. He might not be her Alpha, but he was still a dominant wolf. Yes, she hadn't lowered her eyes before, but she'd been rocked a bit since Adam had told the others of her future. She didn't want to antagonize anyone when Gideon clearly wanted to show his power. Previously, everything had been casual; now it clearly was not.

Kade growled beside her. "Gideon."

The Talon Alpha snorted, not smiling, but moved his gaze. "It's fun to see how she reacts."

"She's my daughter and the future Enforcer."

"*She* is right here, so how about you answer my question?"

Jasper chuckled by her side, and Gina wondered how quickly she could reach the nearest window and jump. It couldn't be that far. She wouldn't die from the fall or anything, and she'd be able to run home.

Quickly.

"Mating," Kade put in, the laughter in his eyes fading, "is only a small part of the problem. When we sent Caym back to hell with the other demons, it changed the power structure within the Packs as well as outside them. The Centrals who fought against us died because they'd lost their souls to the demon. The Centrals that had hidden from the old Alphas ended up being lone wolves. They're not truly a Pack yet because the goddess hasn't made anyone an Alpha."

"Then you have the Redwoods, with a hierarchy shift

within the younger generation," Gideon said. "And the Talons' new power dynamic is only fifteen years old, and we haven't had a mating in long enough that it's starting to worry us."

"Not that you'd say that to the rest of the Pack," Mitchell mumbled.

"It's best they don't know," Gideon said, the sounds of an old argument telling Gina there was more going on here than what they revealed.

Interesting.

"There aren't any matings between our two Packs, and I know the trust isn't fully there," Kade put in then sighed. "I don't know how to fix that myself. I don't think I can."

"You're the Alpha," Jasper said calmly. "If you *tell* them to get along with the other wolves, they will, and for the most part, they have. But it isn't as authentic as if they find that trust on their own. We've let them go this long on their own, but now, I think we need to find another way to have our Packs more entwined."

The dark-eyed wolf came forward then. "You've seen something," he growled.

Dear goddess. His voice.

Her wolf perked, and she shoved her down. This wasn't the time.

"We've seen...something, Quinn," Kade answered.

Quinn. That was his name.

Sexy.

And again, *so* not the time.

Tattered Loyalties

From New York Times Bestselling Author Carrie Ann Ryan's Talon Pack Series

When the great war between the Redwoods and the Centrals occurred three decades ago, the Talon Pack risked their lives for the side of good. After tragedy struck, Gideon Brentwood became the Alpha of the Talons. But the Pack's stability is threatened, and he's forced to take mate—only the one fate puts in his path is the woman he shouldn't want.

Though the daughter of the Redwood Pack's Beta, Brie Jamenson has known peace for most of her life. When she finds the man who could be her mate, she's shocked to discover Gideon is the Alpha wolf of the Talon Pack. As a submissive, her strength lies in her heart, not her claws. But if her new Pack disagrees or disapproves, the consequences could be fatal.

As the worlds Brie and Gideon have always known begin to shift, they must face their challenges together in order to help their Pack and seal their bond. But when the Pack is threatened from the inside, Gideon doesn't know who he can trust and Brie's life could be forfeit in the crossfire. It will take the strength of an Alpha and the courage of his mate to realize where true loyalties lie.

Delicate Ink

From New York Times Bestselling Author Carrie Ann Ryan's Montgomery Ink Series

On the wrong side of thirty, Austin Montgomery is ready to settle down. Unfortunately, his inked sleeves and scruffy beard isn't the suave business appearance some women crave. Only finding a woman who can deal with his job, as a tattoo artist and owner of Montgomery Ink, his seven meddling siblings, and his own gruff attitude won't be easy.

Finding a man is the last thing on Sierra Elder's mind. A recent transplant to Denver, her focus is on opening her own boutique. Wanting to cover up scars that run deeper than her flesh, she finds in Austin a man that truly gets to her—in more ways than one.

Although wary, they embark on a slow, tempestuous burn of a relationship. When blasts from both their pasts intrude on their present, however, it will take more than a promise of what could be to keep them together.

Dust of My Wings

From New York Times Bestselling Author Carrie Ann Ryan's Dante's Circle Series

Humans aren't as alone as they choose to believe. Every human possesses a trait of supernatural that lays dormant within their genetic make-up. Centuries of diluting and breeding have allowed humans to think they are alone and untouched by magic. But what happens when something changes?

Neat freak lab tech, Lily Banner lives her life as any ordinary human. She's dedicated to her work and loves to hang out with her friends at Dante's Circle, their local bar. When she discovers a strange blue dust at work she meets a handsome stranger holding secrets – and maybe her heart. But after a close call with a thunderstorm, she may not be as ordinary as she thinks.

Shade Griffin is a warrior angel sent to Earth to protect the supernaturals' secrets. One problem, he can't stop leaving dust in odd places around town. Now he has to find every ounce of his dust and keep the presence of the supernatural a secret. But after a close encounter with a sexy lab tech and a lightning quick connection, his millennia old loyalties may shift and he could lose more than just his wings in the chaos.

Warning: Contains a sexy angel with a choice to make and a green-eyed lab tech who dreams of a dark-winged stranger. Oh yeah, and a shocking spark that's sure to leave them begging for more.

Charmed Spirits

From New York Times Bestselling Author Carrie Ann Ryan's Holiday Montana Series

Jordan Cross has returned to Holiday, Montana after eleven long years to clear out her late aunt's house, put it on the market, and figure out what she wants to do with the rest of her life. Soon, she finds herself facing the town that turned its back on her because she was different. Because being labeled a witch in a small town didn't earn her many friends...especially when it wasn't a lie.

Matt Cooper has lived in Holiday his whole life. He's

perfectly content being a bachelor alongside his four single brothers in a very small town. After all, the only woman he'd ever loved ran out on him without a goodbye. But now Jordan's back and just as bewitching as ever. Can they rekindle their romance with a town set against them?

Warning: Contains an intelligent, sexy witch with an attitude and drop-dead gorgeous man who likes to work with his hands, holds a secret that might scare someone, and really, *really*, likes table tops for certain activities. Enough said.

Printed in Great B
by Amazon.co.uk,
Marston Gate